Ruby ▌▌▌▌▌▌▌▌ m®

#4 Visitors Welcome

7 56 - 8:26

By Deirdre Black
Illustrated by Artful Doodlers

PUFFIN
CANADA

PUFFIN CANADA

Published by the Penguin Group

Penguin Group (Canada), 90 Eglinton Avenue East, Suite 700, Toronto, Ontario, Canada
M4P 2Y3 (a division of Pearson Canada Inc.)

Penguin Group (USA) Inc., 375 Hudson Street, New York, New York 10014, U.S.A.
Penguin Books Ltd, 80 Strand, London WC2R 0RL, England
Penguin Ireland, 25 St Stephen's Green, Dublin 2, Ireland (a division of Penguin Books Ltd)
Penguin Group (Australia), 250 Camberwell Road, Camberwell, Victoria 3124, Australia
(a division of Pearson Australia Group Pty Ltd)
Penguin Books India Pvt Ltd, 11 Community Centre, Panchsheel Park,
New Delhi – 110 017, India
Penguin Group (NZ), 67 Apollo Drive, Rosedale, North Shore 0632, New Zealand
(a division of Pearson New Zealand Ltd)
Penguin Books (South Africa) (Pty) Ltd, 24 Sturdee Avenue, Rosebank,
Johannesburg 2196, South Africa

Penguin Books Ltd, Registered Offices: 80 Strand, London WC2R 0RL, England

Published in Puffin Canada paperback by Penguin Group (Canada), a division of Pearson Canada
Inc., 2008. Simultaneously published in the U.S.A. by Grosset & Dunlap, a division of Penguin
Young Readers Group, 345 Hudson Street, New York, NY 10014.

1 2 3 4 5 6 7 8 9 10 (WEB)

Manufactured in Canada.

LIBRARY AND ARCHIVES CANADA CATALOGUING IN PUBLICATION

Black, Deirdre
Visitors welcome / written by Deirdre Black ; illustrated by Artful Doodlers.

(Ruby Gloom ; bk. #4)
ISBN 978-0-14-316940-6

I. Artful Doodlers Ltd. II. Title. III. Series: Ruby Gloom (Toronto, Ont.) ; bk. 4
PZ7.B52868Vis 2008a   j813'.6   C2008-902750-7

American Library of Congress Cataloging in Publication data available

www.rubygloom.com

Visit the Penguin Group (Canada) website at **www.penguin.ca**

Special and corporate bulk purchase rates available; please see **www.penguin.ca/corporatesales**
or call 1-800-810-3104, ext. 477 or 474

Dear Friend,

Welcome to Gloomsville!

I'm Ruby Gloom, the happiest girl in the world. My friends and I live in a wonderful old mansion. Each of my friends is special in their own way, and I can't wait for you to meet them. I know you'll love them as much as I do.

There's Iris, a one-eyed girl who loves going on wild adventures; Skull Boy, who's always trying to figure out who's in his family tree; Frank and Len, brothers who share a body and a love of loud music; Poe, the smartest crow I know; Misery, a girl with the worst luck in the world; Scaredy Bat, a little bat who's afraid of everything; Boo Boo, a ghost who isn't the least bit scary; and Doom Kitty, my best friend.

My friends and I are always excited when we're faced with something new, but sometimes we can get a little carried away! In this story, a news report about aliens causes a flurry of confusion when we think that Gloomsville is going to have some special visitors from above.

It all worked out in the end, and it's like I always say: A true friend thinks you're a good egg even if you are half-cracked.

Enjoy our story!

Your friend, Ruby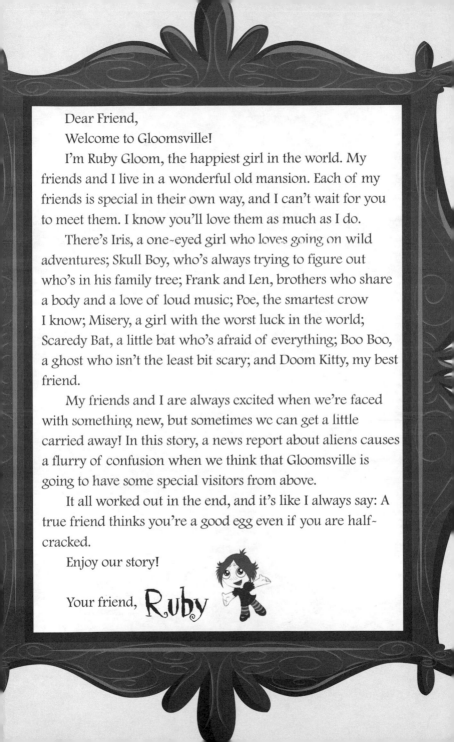

Chapter One

"Any plan is a good plan . . . if it's planned with a friend!"

One morning in Gloomsville, as the moon yawned and waved hello to the rising sun, Poe stepped onto his terrace and stretched. His sleek black feathers fluttered in the chilly morning breeze as he gazed out at the skyline.

"Ah, the cycle continues," Poe said, taking a deep breath. "The sun, the moon, and the stars."

Poe always spoke with an air of poetry. He was a self-professed master stage actor, and his voice had the practiced singsong quality of someone who was always performing.

"And tonight," he went on, "will be a night to

remember forever!" For a few moments, he watched the sun rise. "Well," he finally muttered, pulling out his big pocket watch and checking the time, "I'd better get ready."

Meanwhile, Ruby Gloom was serving breakfast in the big, warm kitchen. She lived in a large, old mansion in Gloomsville with all of her friends. That morning, Iris, Skull Boy, and Scaredy Bat were all sitting around the kitchen table. Ruby's red hair bounced lightly as she ran back and forth between the big fire-pit stove and the table.

Ruby loved to cook and bake, but she especially loved making treats for her friends—and they loved eating the treats she made.

"Good morning," Ruby said as she brought over a basket of warm muffins.

Scaredy Bat jumped a little as Ruby put a giant muffin on his plate. "Oh, good morning, Ruby," he said, looking sleepy. "I guess I am still not totally awake." He rubbed his eyes with his little wings and yawned.

"Yeah," Iris agreed, also yawning. "Scaredy and I were up late last night listening to stories on the radio."

"Ooh, I love radio shows," Skull Boy said, getting to his feet and hiking up his dark gray jeans. "I think I really have a great voice for radio, don't you?" He cleared his throat and continued in a very deep voice, like a radio announcer: "And now, radio listeners, presenting the Skull Boy Story Hour! In today's adventure, the evil Captain Canker captures our hero, Skull Boy! Can Skull Boy escape? Or is he *doomed*?"

Ruby's graceful black cat, Doom Kitty, was curled up on the floor near his feet. At the word *doomed*, she opened one eye and looked up at Skull Boy reproachfully.

"No offense, Doom Kitty," Skull Boy said in his normal voice. Then he finished in his radio voice again. "Tune in next week for the Skull Boy Story Hour to find out!"

The others applauded. "You sound just like the guy on the radio!" Ruby exclaimed. "That was great!"

"Oh, yes," Scaredy Bat agreed. "You certainly have a real talent for storytelling. Even if your story was a little frightening."

Skull Boy took a little bow. "Hey," he said, smiling and looking up in thought, "maybe I'm related to a great radio host, like Boris Karloff or Orson Welles!"

"Well," Iris said, her eye twinkling with excitement, "if you'd like, you can join us tonight. Scaredy and I are going to listen to some more radio stories after supper." She jumped up and began to run around, cleaning up the kitchen.

"Oh, I can't tonight," Skull Boy said excitedly. "Ruby and I are working on a big movie script, *An American in Gloomsville*. It's going to take all day."

"Are you sure?" Iris asked temptingly. "I'm going to make ginger cookies and spiced milk!"

"Sorry, Iris," Ruby replied. "We're working on the big musical number. It's a pretty huge project."

Iris stopped, took a sip of juice, and wiped her mouth. "That's okay. There are radio stories on every night," she explained. "You can join us another time!"

Just then, Poe came into the kitchen. "Good morning, good morning!" he said. The others could immediately see that he was excited.

"Poe!" Iris said. "What's the hubbub all about?"

"Yes, yes, good morning to you all," Poe replied. "Please don't mind me. I just need to look around in here for a few minutes. Tonight is a very big night. A monumental occasion!"

He began poking around the kitchen, looking into corners, behind the stove, and even under the table. "You know," he commented, mostly to himself, "that's not a bad idea. Perhaps I should erect a monument to remember this night for generations to come."

"Um, did you lose something, Poe?" Ruby asked.

But Poe didn't seem to hear her. Instead he stopped in the middle of the kitchen and put his wings on his hips. "Now where did I . . ." he

muttered. The gang watched him for a moment, confused.

Suddenly Poe turned to them and said, "Tonight, dear friends, is a very big night. You will all remember it for the rest of your lives!"

"Poe," Iris said, "what's so special about tonight?"

But Poe winked at her. "Just keep your eyes on the skies!" he said mysteriously. "Now I must find it . . ." he added, and then he rushed out of the kitchen.

"Poe sure can be . . . weird sometimes," Skull Boy remarked.

"Frightening!" Scaredy Bat agreed.

"I'm sure he just has a lot on his mind," Ruby said. "He'll explain when he's ready."

Chapter Two

"A good story keeps you
guessing . . . but don't forget
to eat your cookies, too!"

That evening, Iris was bouncing with excitement in her favorite high-backed chair in the Great Hall in front of a roaring fire.

Iris was listening to a radio show—a nerve-wracking, terrifying radio show. And she was shivering with anticipation.

"Several large flying disks were spotted in the sky moments ago," said the story's newscaster character. "Officials are en route to the scene now."

Wow, Iris thought. *This radio show is awesome.*

"The authorities have made contact with the aliens," the newscaster character continued. "We are being told that hundreds of ships are on the way now. Our reporter is on the scene."

The show cut to the reporter character. "That's correct, Jim," the reporter said. She sounded very excited and had to speak loudly to be heard over the zooms, booms, bangs, and clangs in the background.

"It sounds so realistic," Iris said to herself as she leaned forward in her chair, thrilled to her toes. "I wonder where Scaredy Bat is. He's missing the show!"

The reporter

continued. "As a matter of fact, looking up now, I can see dozens . . . no, hundreds of ships closing in."

"Can you describe the scene, Mary?" the newscaster said.

"Well, Jim," she replied, "the sky is filled with huge, mysterious, shiny disks. I am surrounded by concerned citizens, and I can hardly hear over the noise."

"Sounds terrible," the newscaster replied.

"It is, Jim," the reporter agreed. Iris shivered. The reporter went on: "This could be . . . the end of the world as we know it! Back to you, Jim."

"Thank you for that eyewitness report," the newscaster said.

"And remember, ladies and gentleman, the public is warned to stay indoors," the narrator said. "This is most likely a full-scale alien invasion!"

Suddenly, the show's general radio

announcer cut in. "And we will be right back after these messages."

"Ugh," Iris said. "Awful timing, Mister Narrator. Just when the real invasion was about to begin!"

Iris sighed and leaned back in her chair to wait for the commercial break to end. She had a plate of ginger cookies on her lap and a tall mug of spiced milk in her hand, but both were still untouched. The story had been so exciting, she hadn't even thought to take a sip or a bite.

"Hello, radio listeners!" began the first commercial. "Are your dogs, cats, lizards, parakeets, meerkats, hedgehogs, and buffaloes as happy as they could be?"

Iris leaned forward. She was always very interested in anything to do with animal care. Thinking about Squig, her giant flying pet worm, she replied, "I think so . . ."

"Well," the commercial's narrator continued,

"they're probably not, unless you're buying your pet food from the finest pet-food maker in Gloomsville . . ."

Iris was back on the edge of her seat.

"The A-one, top-quality animal-feed maker," the narrator went on, "Great Grub!"

"Whew," Iris sighed with relief. "Squig always eats Great Grub. He wouldn't be happy with anything less."

Smiling, she finally picked up a cookie and took a big bite. "Squig sure does love Great Grub," she said to herself. "Why, Squig looks forward to mealtime more than—"

"Whoops!" she said, jumping up. "Squig's mealtime was twenty minutes ago!"

As she leaped from the chair, her cookies and milk fell from her lap. The mug and plate smashed onto the rug and shattered, sending cookies and splashing milk in every direction. As Iris's foot hit the milky wet rug, she slipped.

"Yeep!" she shrieked as she flipped through the air, landing on her feet. "I'm good! No worries!" She glanced at the big clock. Squig would be getting hungry—very hungry.

I'll clean that up when I get back, she thought, glancing at the mess she'd made. *I don't want to keep Squig waiting any longer for his dinner.* And with that, she ran off to feed her pet.

In his bedroom, Poe was searching through his closet. Clothes, costumes, boxes, and bags fell all around him—and sometimes right on him. Poe didn't pay them any mind, though. He was too focused on finding something.

"Now, where did I put it?" he said, his head

almost buried in a heap of old clothes, stage costumes, and suitcases.

"Not in there," he decided as he stood up and turned around. "This night will be totally ruined if I can't find it."

He thought hard for a few seconds, then burst out, "Perhaps the old steamer trunk!"

Poe strode across the room to the foot of his bed, where he kept his old trunk. It was far bigger than he was, made of deep brown wood with brass trimming and a big brass lock. It was covered in stickers from many cities all over the globe, Milwaukee to Moscow. He ran his hand along the top, admiring all the stickers.

"Istanbul, London, New York, Tokyo, Madrid . . . aaah, Paris," he said, longingly. "The City of Lights! The places this trunk has been."

As he stood up, he screwed up his face and added, "If only I could have gone, too." Then he shrugged. "That would have been nice," Poe said to himself, then shouted, "Edgar! Allen!"

Poe's two tall brothers strode into the room and stood waiting next to him.

"Ah, there you are," Poe said. "I require my key ring."

Edgar opened his long black coat and reached deep into an inside pocket. He pulled out a gold chain. Allen took hold of the chain as well, and the two tall crows unraveled foot after foot of it. After several minutes, as Poe gazed down at the trunk, smiling, the brothers finally reached the end of the chain.

And there, at the end of the chain, was a great big key ring. It had at least fifty keys on it, some small and some huge, and each one had a *P* on it. Edgar held up the key ring, and Poe flipped through the keys until he came to the very smallest one: a small silver key with a tiny *P* on it.

"Ah," Poe said, taking the key ring from his

brothers, "the *P* stands for 'Poe's trunk,' you see. Whereas this *P*," he added, touching one of the largest keys on the ring, "stands for 'Poe's piggy bank.'"

Edgar and Allen glanced at each other.

"It helps to keep things organized," Poe explained. "That's very important when you have a mind as complex as mine."

Sighing, Poe swung open the trunk. It was filled to the top with old costumes and papers and little odds and ends. Poe grabbed one costume off the top and held it up.

"From my role as King Mortimer in the play by Lord Fezzington Shortbottom!" he said nobly as he stepped into the costume.

Poe thrust one hand into the air and stuck out his chin. "Alack!" he said. His voice was commanding and deep. "Wherefore hast thine gone, m'lady? For 'tis . . . er . . . not haveth . . . or . . . Mine eyes hath not . . . forsooth . . . Er."

He scratched his chin. "Hmm," Poe muttered. Then he waved, dismissing the forgotten dialogue. "Well, so on and so forth. It's been quite a while."

Poe pulled off the costume and dug deep into the trunk full of fabrics. "Well now," he said. "Back to the hunt. Where *did* I put it?"

He reached farther into the huge trunk until his head was completely buried. Within a few minutes, half his body was inside the trunk. And soon he was totally lost, covered in old fabric and clothes. Edgar and Allen, seeing that their brother would be occupied for some time, left Poe to his search.

Poe was still rummaging around at the bottom of the trunk when a strong wind whooshed through the open window and blew the trunk lid closed.

"Er . . ." Poe said, realizing that the trunk was suddenly much darker. "Hello?"

No one replied.

"Is anyone there?" Poe added.

Still, no one replied.

"I say, I seem to be locked inside this trunk," Poe shouted, much louder now. But still, no one replied. "Edgar? Allen?"

"Drat."

Chapter Three

"Don't believe everything
you hear . . . or fear!"

Scaredy Bat walked quickly through the house, on his way to the Great Hall. Shadows loomed over him as the moonlight shone through the tall windows all around him.

Scaredy Bat never liked to be on his own after dark—not to mention before dark, during dark, and between dark. Which is why he had made plans to meet up with Iris to listen to some radio shows. He would have company until he got sleepy since she would be in the Great Hall listening to her favorite radio programs all night.

Scaredy Bat should have met Iris over an hour ago, but he had been reading one of his favorite books—*The Bat Who Came in from the Cold*—while lounging in his hammock, and he had simply lost track of time.

Oh, dear. I am so late! Scaredy thought as he walked into the Great Hall. *I hope Iris has not given up on me. I was so looking forward to a nice relaxing evening—safe and sound with a good friend and some nice, non-scary radio shows.*

But as Scaredy reached the blaring radio and the pair of high-backed chairs near the fire, he was surprised and disappointed to find both chairs empty.

"Hello there? Iris?" Scaredy said. "Is anyone here?" Scaredy peered into the darkness, hoping Iris was just nearby in the shadows.

"I guess she couldn't wait any longer,"

Scaredy said, annoyed with himself. "Oh, why am I so late?"

But something bothered him more than usual about the empty room. "Hmm, how very odd," he muttered. "Why would the radio still be on if Iris had gone to bed?"

Scaredy walked toward the radio, thinking he might as well turn it off if no one was going to listen. But in front of one of the chairs, he stepped in something wet, and shivers went up his spine. He looked down and saw a puddle of milk, broken cookies, and a shattered mug.

"Oh my, oh

my," he muttered, shaking. "What happened here?"

He reached down and picked up a broken piece of the mug. "A broken mug of milk," he whispered. "And ginger cookies?"

Something must have happened to Iris, Scaredy thought. *Something terrible!* Suddenly, a voice on the radio caught his attention. A newscaster was speaking, and he seemed very upset. "I repeat, we have confirmed this is a full-scale invasion by aliens."

Scaredy's eyes opened wide with fear.

"At least one hundred ships have been sighted by our reporter on the scene," the newscaster went on. "Townspeople are gathering together to defend themselves."

Scaredy dropped the piece of mug. "I am suddenly feeling quite faint," he muttered.

The newscaster went on: "Once again, we are advising the public to stay indoors. Lock your

doors. Be on the lookout for anything unusual—
anything at all!"

"Aliens!" Scaredy Bat shrieked. He looked
down at the mess of cookies and broken mug
and milk. The fire roared and crackled, sending
huge shadows over the room.

The radio leaned forward, toward Scaredy,
as the newscaster went on: "I repeat, if you
see anything unusual at all, notify someone at
once!"

Scaredy looked around. "Broken mug," he
counted off, "scattered cookies, and one missing
friend . . . That is very unusual. What if . . . Iris
. . . has been . . ."

Scaredy put his little hand over his mouth.
He could hardly say the word: "Abducted!"

"This just in . . ." the newscaster went on.
Scaredy heard the newscaster grab a sheet of
paper from someone and clear his throat. "We
are now receiving numerous reports of citizens

being abducted . . . right out of their homes!"

"Oh my!" Scaredy said, almost shouting. "Then Iris was abducted!"

Scaredy stood for a moment. "I have to get help."

Then he took a deep, deep breath and shouted, "Ruuuuby!"

Chapter Four

> "Talk things over with friends. . .
> Even if it doesn't solve anything,
> you'll be with friends!"

Ruby Gloom and her friend Skull Boy sat together at the kitchen table. The script to *An American in Gloomsville* was spread all over the table. Doom Kitty prowled around at their feet.

"Sure is nice and quiet this evening,"

Skull Boy said as he looked over the dance moves they had written down so far.

"Yup," Ruby agreed. "Nice and quiet."

Suddenly, a scream shattered the silence.

"Ruuuuby!"

Ruby sat up and listened. "Is that . . ." she started.

Skull Boy nodded as he got up from the table to peek into the hallway. "Yup," he said, spotting Scaredy Bat running breathlessly through the mansion.

"Ruuuby!" the little bat shouted again.

"In here, Scaredy Bat," Skull Boy called. "Is something wrong?"

Scaredy practically dove into the kitchen and went straight for the table—to hide under it. Doom Kitty had to leap out of the way at the last moment to avoid being knocked over.

"I'll say something is wrong," Scaredy said through his chattering teeth. "Broken mug and

. . . I mean, the aliens. And cookies! *Cookies everywhere!*"

Ruby and Skull Boy tucked their heads under the table. "It's okay, Scaredy. We're here with you. You can come out of there," Ruby said.

"Yeah," added Skull Boy. "We'll protect you from the alien cookies. Nothing can get you in here."

Scaredy Bat shook his head. "That's not what the radio said," he stammered. "The radio said people were being taken right out of their *homes*!" And he tucked his head under his wing.

Ruby and Skull Boy glanced at each other. "The radio?" Ruby asked.

"People being taken out of their homes?" Skull Boy added. "What are you talking about, Scaredy Bat?"

With a light laugh, Ruby crawled under the table with Scaredy. "Start at the beginning, Scaredy Bat. What happened?"

Scaredy peeked out from under his wing. "Well, Iris and I had planned to listen to some radio shows this evening by the fire," he began.

"Iris loves those radio shows," Ruby said. "She was excited about tonight's program."

"Yeah, I remember her mentioning it over breakfast," Skull Boy noted.

"Well," Scaredy went on, "I went down to the Great Hall to meet her . . ." And he went on, with much shivering, to relay the story of finding the broken mug, the spilled milk, the cookie pieces, and the alien invasion news report on the radio.

"So," he finally finished, "it is clear that Iris has been abducted by aliens!"

By now, Skull Boy and Doom Kitty were also under the table.

"Maybe you're overreacting, Scaredy Bat," Ruby replied after a moment. "Iris might be just fine. Maybe she just made a mess by accident."

Skull Boy nodded. "Right," he said. "It's probably nothing."

"Nothing?" Scaredy said. "But what about the aliens?"

Skull Boy started to stand and bonked his head on the table. "Ow," he said. "I don't believe aliens are landing here."

"*Invading!* Not landing. *Invading!*" Scaredy Bat corrected.

"Right, invading," Skull Boy said, carefully climbing out from under the table. "But let's see what the radio says."

Skull Boy walked over to the kitchen radio

and switched it on. As the four of them waited with anticipation, the radio crackled, and sound filled the room.

". . . full-scale invasion," the newscaster was saying. "We are advising the public to remain inside, with the doors and windows locked."

"I can't believe it!" Skull Boy said.

The newscaster went on: "Our reporter on the scene has sighted no fewer than one hundred alien ships. They are beginning to land."

"Aliens really *are* landing here!" Skull Boy said with a smile.

"Why are you smiling?" Scaredy Bat asked, shocked.

"Are you kidding? This is the most exciting thing that's ever happened," he said.

"I don't know . . ." Ruby said. "But if aliens really are landing, we better be ready." Doom Kitty nodded.

Scaredy Bat finally climbed out from under

the table. "Most definitely," he said. "I will gather food and water. We can barricade ourselves in the basement right away."

"Barricade ourselves?" Skull Boy said, shocked.

"In the basement?" Ruby said, confused.

"Yes," Scaredy Bat said. "We will be safest from abduction in the basement."

"What's all the food and water for?" Skull Boy asked.

"We may have to be there for a very long time," Scaredy replied, his arms already full of jars of Ruby's homemade peach and pear preserves.

"Good thinking,

Scaredy," Skull Boy said, grabbing a few pies
Ruby had baked that morning.

"Oh, Scaredy Bat," Ruby said. "That's not
what I meant by being ready."

"It isn't?" Scaredy Bat asked.

"It isn't?" echoed Skull Boy.

Ruby shook her head. "No!" she said. "I bet
if aliens really are landing here, they're not
invading at all."

"But, the radio—" Scaredy said. "And Iris is
missing!"

"I'm sure Iris is fine," Ruby replied, digging
around in the cupboards for something. "But if
the aliens have traveled all this way to visit—"

"Visit?" Skull Boy asked.

". . . they'll probably be very hungry when
they get here," Ruby finished. "We should be
good hosts. I'd better get baking."

"Baking?!" Skull Boy and Scaredy Bat said in
unison.

"Yup," Ruby replied. "And I better start right now. If that reporter is right, it's going to take a lot of doom cakes to feed them all!"

Skull Boy shook his head. "I'm calling a house meeting!" he said.

While Scaredy was recounting his story to Ruby and Skull Boy, Poe was digging through some old boxes in the garage. Edgar and Allen had finally come to check on him and let him out of the trunk.

"I know I put it here someplace," he muttered to himself. His excitement from that morning still shone through. "But where . . . ?"

His eyes glimmered. "Aha!" he said, spotting a long, big box. "That must be it! I'll be ready for tonight in no time at all."

He waddled over to the box he'd seen and struggled to pick it up. "Dear me," he said. "I don't remember it being quite so heavy."

He quickly flexed his wings and gave his muscle a squeeze. "Oh my," he whispered. "I really ought to get back to my weight training. I've gone right to pot, haven't I?"

Sizing up the box, Poe spat on each hand, rubbed them together, and grabbed hold of it. "Clean and jerk," he said. "Nothing . . . unggghh . . . to it . . ."

The box budged slightly, but his hands slipped and he fell backward into a pile of sawdust. "Aahh!" he shouted, landing with a thud.

Coughing, Poe got to his feet and stumbled back to the box. Now the top had torn clean off and Poe could see what was inside it.

"What's this?" he said. The box contained dozens of swords.

"Why," Poe went on, a faraway look on his face, "it's my old collection of stage swords, from my time with the London Dramatic Opera

Company. How wonderful."

He picked one up and struck a fencing stance. "En garde!" he commanded to his imaginary fencing partner.

Slash! Stab! Parry! Poe danced around the shed, fencing with the shadows and moving gracefully.

"Touché!" he cried, thrusting his sword forward. Then, for a grand finale, he raised the sword high above his head and, with a great "Hiiii-yaaaaahhh," rushed his invisible enemy . . .

until he tripped over a pile of lumber. The crow tumbled through the air, knocked loose a shelf full of paint cans, and landed with a great crash on a heap of old rags. A single rake fell slowly from its place and bonked him on the head.

Sitting up, Poe shook the stars from his eyes and rubbed his head. "Drat."

Chapter Five

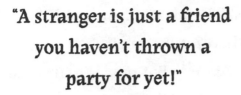

"A stranger is just a friend
you haven't thrown a
party for yet!"

"What's going on?" Frank said as he and
Len strode into the Great Hall. Frank and Len
were brothers who shared a body and a love of
playing loud music. Skull Boy and Misery were
standing by the fire, and Scaredy Bat was under
one of the high-backed chairs, shaking, which
wasn't too unusual.

"Yeah, Ruby said Skull Boy was calling a
house meeting," Len added. "So what's the big
emergency?"

"Oh, it's no big deal," Skull Boy said.
"Nothing we'd want to interrupt songwriting

for." Then, turning to face the brothers, he added in a shout, "It's only . . . *aliens from outer space landing in Gloomsville!*"

"Aliens?" Frank and Len replied together. "Landing here? Awesome!"

"And," Scaredy Bat piped up from under a chair, "abducting Iris!"

Just then, Ruby came in carrying a big mixing bowl. Her face was covered in flour and she was stirring furiously. "I couldn't find Poe anywhere," she said with a shrug.

"Hmm," Skull Boy said, stroking his chin. "Come to think of it, I haven't seen Poe since this morning in the kitchen."

"Oh, yeah!" Ruby replied, remembering the crow's weird appearance during breakfast. "He was

looking for something."

"And he mentioned something big would happen tonight!" Skull Boy noted.

"He also said 'keep your eyes on the skies,'" Scaredy Bat pointed out.

Skull Boy snapped. "That's it!" he said. "Poe must have known about the alien invasion . . . somehow!"

Ruby nodded. "He's always looking at the stars," she pointed out. "I bet he spotted their ships days ago, and went out to greet them."

Skull Boy agreed. "That's probably it exactly," he said. "And, since no one has seen him since this morning, he was probably abducted, too."

"Eep!" Scaredy Bat said, and tucked his head under his wing.

"Oh, Skull Boy," Ruby said shaking her head. "I'm sure Iris and Poe are fine, even if they are with the aliens. I bet the aliens are totally friendly!"

"Ruby's right," Misery said. "Aliens are friendly. At least, the ones my family met."

"Your family met aliens?" Skull Boy asked in amazement.

Misery nodded slowly. "You know, come to think of it, I'm not surprised the aliens are coming to Gloomsville," Misery said as she dropped into a chair by the fire. "But they're not coming for Iris and Poe. They're coming for me."

"For you?" Ruby asked. She was now deftly holding a cake in one hand and using her other hand to spread bright orange icing all over it.

"Why would they be here for you, Misery?" Frank asked.

"My great-aunt Moana met them the last time the aliens came to visit," Misery replied. She sighed. "She lived out in the desert. Their big spaceship crushed Moana's house."

"That's awful!" Ruby said.

Misery shrugged. "Moana made friends with the aliens, and they said they would come back to visit our family again. But no one believed her. Everyone else said that the spaceships were just weather balloons."

"I knew they were friendly!" Ruby said. By now she had iced three large cakes. Doom Kitty was balancing a fourth on her tail while Ruby mixed up a batch of yellow icing.

"They'll probably crush the mansion," Misery noted.

Scaredy Bat stuck his head out and said, "Eep."

"Don't be afraid, Scaredy," Frank said.

"Right," Len agreed, picking up his guitar. "We're excited about the aliens!" He played a few licks on his guitar. "We should write a song to welcome them when they get here."

"Great idea, dude," Frank said. He started improvising along with Len's guitar playing:

"Space dudes, come down in your big UFO;
You remember Misery's aunt from sixty years ago!
Ruby made cakes, so you'll be happy to meet her;
And after the party, I'll take you to our leader."

"Great song!" Ruby said, wiping her brow and leaving a trail of bright yellow frosting. "It'll be perfect for playing at my Welcome to Gloomsville party!"

"Thanks, Ruby," Frank said.

Ruby looked around at the cakes she had iced.

Doom Kitty swayed under the weight of the cakes balanced on her head, her back, and the two balancing on her tail.

"I better get back to the kitchen to make some more cakes," Ruby said with a sigh. "Hundreds of ships! So much to do!"

Poe was, in fact, in the mansion. As the kids discussed the aliens, he was directly below them in the cellar, rummaging around in old boxes.

"Wherever did I put it?" he muttered to himself as he searched.

Suddenly, he spotted a long, worn cardboard box on a high shelf. "Aha!" he proclaimed, and he pulled over a stepladder to reach it.

"There we are," Poe said, reaching on his tiptoes from the very top step of the ladder. "Just a few . . . more . . . inches . . . and . . ."

He stretched the tips of his wings to their

very limits, finally managing to tip the big box off of the shelf. "There!" he said. Just then, Poe's box, plus all of the other boxes on the shelf, came tumbling down, knocking Poe off of his ladder and onto the floor.

"Achoo!" Poe sneezed as dust from the old boxes tickled his beak, followed closely by, "Ow."

Staggering back to his feet, Poe found the box he had been hoping to get down and opened it. "Now then," he said, brightening.  "Here we are—Wait. What's this?"

And he pulled out a huge beach umbrella. "This isn't what I wanted at all!" he said. And just then, the big umbrella sprung open in his hand, sending him flying back into the dusty heap of boxes.

"Drat," he said. "Perhaps . . . the attic . . ."

Chapter Six

> "Preparation is very
> important, especially if it's
> followed by *celebration!*"

Skull Boy, now in his full general's regalia,
paced thoughtfully before the fire. He tapped a

baton into his open
hand as he walked.
"Hmm . . ." he said.

"I am not so
sure about having
a party for the
aliens," Scaredy
Bat said timidly. He
was following close
behind Skull Boy.

Skull Boy nodded, then stopped suddenly. Scaredy Bat was walking so closely behind him that he knocked right into Skull Boy, and they both fell into a heap on the rug.

"The time has come for action!" Skull Boy shouted as he stood up again, thrusting his forefinger into the air.

"Yes!" Scaredy Bat agreed. "Action!" The little bat got up from the rug, too. "One question, though, please, if I may," he added meekly.

"Yes, Private?" Skull Boy asked sternly.

"Um, yes, sir," Scaredy Bat said. "Well . . . does action, perhaps, include hiding in the basement?"

"Hiding?" Skull Boy said. "Generals do not hide! They react swiftly! They give orders! They are cool and commanding in a crisis! Like the great Napoleon Bonaparte!" Skull Boy smiled. "I must be related to Napoleon . . . or some great military leader."

"Oh, dear," Scaredy replied, and swallowed deeply.

"We must protect the mansion," Skull Boy went on, pacing again. "We'll start by building a barricade."

"A barricade?" Ruby said as she came in. She was carrying a big banner, three cans of paint, and a ladder. Doom Kitty came in behind her with a paintbrush in tail, and Frank and Len were behind her carrying their guitars and amps.

"We must secure the perimeter!" Skull Boy replied, again thrusting his finger into

the air. "It's what any great general would do! We'll need sandbags . . ."

"Sandbags?" Len said, scratching his head.

"Protection is a good plan," Scaredy Bat said, finally feeling a little safer. "Please listen to the general—I mean, Skull Boy."

"Once the mansion is secure, we can begin a commando offensive to recover our missing troops," Skull Boy went on.

"A commando offensive?" Scaredy asked. "Oh, this is beginning to sound quite dangerous."

"Danger is my middle name!" Skull Boy replied surely. "Under the protection of night, we will attack the alien outpost. We'll need someone to move in and take down their defenses, and someone else to stay here and wait for the 'all-clear.'"

Len stood up solemnly. "I'll go," he said. "Frank can take the all-clear signal here, where it's safe."

Frank shook his head. "Len, that's ridiculous," he said. "Think about it: I'm older, so—"

"Guys," Ruby said, interrupting the brothers. She was holding a paintbrush in her hand; yellow, orange, and black paint splotches dotted her entire face. "I'm sure Iris is fine. Knowing her, she probably just went down to the landing site with Squig already."

Frank nodded. "She does like an adventure," he said.

"Yup," Len agreed. "She's always the first one to show up at an alien landing site."

"And you heard Poe earlier. He had big plans for the night," Ruby added. "So I'm sure he's fine, too. And, besides, we have a party to plan!"

Skull Boy shook his head. "We must prepare for battle!" he insisted.

"No, we *must* finish writing our song, 'I'll Take You to Our Leader'!" Frank and Len rebutted.

Ruby stood up and shook her paintbrush at the others. Yellow and orange paint splattered everywhere. "Oops, sorry," she said, "We *must* set up for the Welcome to Gloomsville party!"

Scaredy Bat, meanwhile, had wandered over to the window. "Please, my friends," he said, "come over to the window. It is of the utmost importance."

The others glared at one another but joined Scaredy Bat at the window.

"Tell me," Scaredy said, sounding terrified. "Have there always been those hundreds of streaking lights in the sky over Gloomsville?"

"Spaceships!" Frank and Len

said. "But the song isn't done!"

"They're here *already*!" Skull Boy said. "But the defenses are not ready!"

"*Hundreds* of ships!" Ruby agreed. "And the party isn't set up!"

Scaredy Bat nodded. "*That* is what I suspected," he said, and fainted from fright.

Poe was sifting through all of the stuff in the mansion's attic. It was filled with boxes and trunks and old suitcases. The shelves on the walls were lined with dusty old books, and there were cobwebs everywhere. The gang rarely went up to the attic, so over the years it had become filled with forgotten treasures . . . and dust.

"Achoo!" Poe sneezed as he searched through every box, trunk, and suitcase.

"This is the last place it could possibly be," Poe said to himself, beginning to worry he might not find what he was looking for. "I simply *must* find . . . ah . . . it . . . ahCHOO!"

The power of the sneeze sent Poe flying backward ten feet, into a heap of old clothes. He landed with a thud.

Getting to his feet, Poe shook his head and rubbed his sore back. "Drat."

Chapter Seven

"Keep friends around
when things go bump in
the night."

"Put the radio back on," Len said.

"Right," Frank added. "They may have some updates."

Misery switched it on. Everyone was on edge as the radio sputtered and whistled, then, after a few seconds of static, clicked to life.

"I'm here at the landing site," the reporter on the radio said. "There are now hundreds of ships hovering overhead."

"That must be what we saw outside!" Skull Boy pointed out.

Ruby, meanwhile, had set up a ladder in the

corner and was busy hanging streamers. "What do you think of these colors?" she asked, but the others were too intent on the radio story to pay her any attention.

"Do not attempt to approach the aliens," the newscaster explained. "We don't know how dangerous they might be."

"Oh dear, oh dear," Scaredy said.

Suddenly, a great *boom* rang out. Everyone jumped.

A terrible scream came from above them.

"What was that?" Scaredy shrieked. He leaped onto Misery's head, shaking.

Another *boom*, and another scream. Len tilted his head.

"I think it came from . . . the attic," Frank said with a puzzled look on his face.

"The aliens must have landed on the roof, and now they're in the attic!" Skull Boy said. "Those screams are probably their battle cry!"

There was another bang and another scream from above them. Soon, they heard a *thump-thump* of feet moving across the floor upstairs.

"Keep quiet, and maybe they won't hear us," Skull Boy whispered as he quickly turned off the radio. "Blasted aliens! They have managed to outsmart me and my brilliant defenses by coming in through the roof!"

Misery sighed. "And they'll probably crush the house with their ships, just like they did to my great-aunt Moana's house."

"Eep!" Scaredy added. "I do not want to be crushed."

"We're doomed!" Frank wailed.

"Done for!" Len agreed.

"And we won't even all be together for the . . . the end!" Scaredy Bat stammered.

"Poor Poe," Skull Boy said, shaking his head. "Abducted by aliens."

"Yes," said Scaredy Bat, sniffling. "And oh, poor Iris!"

"Poor Iris?" Iris said as she came in the back door and walked over to stand beside Misery. "What's going on?"

"Don't you see?" Len replied, turning to Iris. "Iris is missing! Captured!"

"No, Len," Frank said to his brother. Then, without turning around, he replied, "*They're* going to be here any minute, and there's no saving us now. And Poe has been abducted.

And Iris is missing."

"But . . ." Iris said, blinking with confusion. "Guys, I'm here! I'm not missing!"

Suddenly, Skull Boy, Misery, and Scaredy Bat turned to Iris and the brothers with a collective "Shh!"

"Sorry," Iris muttered, still confused. "So . . . *they're* coming, huh?"

"Right," Skull Boy said in a whisper. "And they're already in the attic."

Iris smiled. "This is pretty exciting," she said, and she huddled with the others. Then she noticed Ruby on a ladder in the corner.

"Um," Iris whispered, "what's Ruby doing?"

Skull Boy shrugged. "She's throwing a party for them."

"That sounds like fun," Iris replied.

"There's going to be cake!" Frank added with a smile.

"Shh!" the others hissed.

"I hear footsteps!"

They thumped slowly above them. *Thump, thump, thump.* Soon, they were getting louder.

"The alien is coming downstairs!" Scaredy Bat announced.

"Alien?" Iris asked, but the others didn't seem to hear her.

The friends watched the door. The footsteps grew louder, and louder, and louder.

"It's right outside!" Skull Boy said. "Be ready to defend yourselves, soldiers!"

"Oh, I am not a soldier," Scaredy Bat whispered, and his voice shook. "We surrender, we surrender!" he added in a shout.

The footsteps stopped. The kids saw a shadow in the crack of light under the door.

Suddenly, the door burst open!

The gang screamed.

Chapter Eight

"Things that look weird in
the dark are often familiar
once the lights are on."

The alien stood in the doorway, the bright light from the hall shining behind him. Its huge shadow flooded the room. Everyone started screaming and yelling at once.

"Help us!" Scaredy Bat screamed.

The alien screamed, "Aaaahhh!"

"Attack!" Skull Boy said.

Brang! Frank and Len played several chords loudly on their guitar.

"Aunt Moana says hi!" Misery shouted.

"Aaaahhh!" the alien screamed again.

"Um," Iris added, "hi, Poe."

The others stopped their yells. "Poe?" they all said together.

Iris was right, of course, and after she had switched the lamp on, everyone could see it wasn't an alien at all. It was Poe carrying a big, long wooden crate.

"Er, this is quite heavy," Poe said carefully. "Might I put it down before we continue screaming?"

"We're sorry, Poe. We thought you were the alien!" Misery explained wryly.

"Alien?" Poe asked, leaning the crate against the wall. "What alien?"

"Yeah," Iris added finally. "What alien?"

"The one that landed on the roof," Skull Boy replied.

"On the roof?" Poe said in disbelief.

"You know," Ruby said from her ladder. "The aliens! You knew all about it. You told us to keep our eyes on the skies tonight!"

"They're going to crush the house," Misery said. "Hmm . . ." she added, "I hope they won't be disappointed that my great-aunt Moana isn't here."

"The alien knows your aunt?!" Iris said in wonderment.

"I hope it likes our song," Frank said. Len nodded and strummed his guitar.

"And I hope it likes doom cakes!" Ruby said from the top of her ladder.

"What makes you think there is an alien on the roof?!" Poe shouted over the others. They all stopped chattering and turned to him.

"Play the news for him," Scaredy Bat said, pointing at the radio.

Skull Boy switched the radio back on. The reporter was interviewing the head of the town committee. ". . . emergency," the man said. "Everyone should stay indoors until we can figure out what to do about the invading aliens."

"Oh, dear," Poe said, leaning closer to the radio.

An explosion rang out from the radio. The gang jumped.

"It does sound quite serious," Poe agreed.

"The aliens are dangerous," the man on the radio continued.

"Come to think of it," Poe said, smiling wryly, "this sounds quite familiar!"

The man went on: "This invasion will take its toll . . ."

"On all of us," Poe finished in unison with the man on the radio. He cleared his throat and stepped in front of the radio. Then he struck an actor's dramatic pose.

"In fact," Poe went on, perfectly in time with the man on the radio, "this conflict may mean the end of our fair town."

The others gazed at Poe in disbelief. "How did . . . how did you know what he'd say, Poe?!" Skull Boy asked.

"Simple," Poe said. "This is not a newscast we are listening to, as you seem to believe."

Iris nodded. "Right," she said. "It's a radio show. A story."

"Correct," Poe said, letting the word roll off of his tongue. "It is, in fact, a dramatic reading of the science-fiction classic *They Came from the Sky*, by J. S. Sidney."

"A reading?" Skull Boy said, astonished.

Poe walked over to the bookcase along the far wall and scanned the titles. "Ah," he said, picking up a large volume. He blew the dust off the cover and handed the book to Skull Boy. "See?"

Skull Boy looked at the cover, then flipped through a few pages of the book. "Aliens . . . the concerned citizens . . . a newscaster . . . Poe's

right! It is this book!"

Scaredy Bat wasn't fully convinced. "But all the banging!" he insisted. "And those terrible lights we saw! Oh, dear!" He tucked his head under his wing and fell to the floor.

"Lights?" Poe said. "Oh, you mean the meteor shower!"

"Meteor shower?" Misery asked.

Poe nodded, then picked up the box he had been carrying. "That's right," he said. "Tonight is the most magnificent meteor shower of our century. And the banging upstairs you heard was, regrettably, well . . . me!"

"You?!" the others said in shock.

"Well, yes," Poe said, and he opened the crate. "I was searching high and low . . . for this!" And he held up the biggest, most impressive telescope any of them had ever seen. Once it was set up, the gang could see it was longer than Skull Boy was tall. And it shined and gleamed in the candlelight of the Great Hall, gold tubes and brass knobs and copper legs and glass lenses. It was a most impressive piece of equipment.

"It's my finest telescope," Poe said, smiling proudly. "With it, the properly trained eye could spot a flea on Jupiter."

Poe stepped back from the telescope and fiddled with some of the knobs. The various pieces swung around to and fro, forcing the gang to duck to avoid being bonked in the head.

"I didn't want to watch this meteor shower through one of my everyday telescopes," Poe explained as he adjusted the equipment.

Misery nodded. "Understandable," she said.

"But, Iris," Scaredy Bat said. "The spilled milk and cookies on the floor . . . weren't you attacked?"

Iris shook her head. "Of course not!" she replied. "I just dropped them. I was in a hurry to go feed Squig."

"But you were missing for so long!" Skull Boy pointed out.

Iris shrugged. "You know me and Squig," she said. "We got to playing and, well . . . I sort of forgot about the radio show and the mess I'd left on the rug."

"Well, Iris," Skull Boy said, clapping her on the shoulder, "we're glad you weren't abducted by aliens."

"And you, too, Poe," Len added.

"Yes," Scaredy Bat said, tugging the crow's sleeve, "but we're even gladder you're not an alien *yourself*!"

Chapter Nine

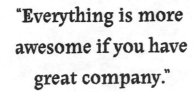

"Everything is more awesome if you have great company."

The gang stood outside gazing at the sky. Great golden, red, green, and blue meteors streaked by overhead. Then the sky was just twinkling stars and black again.

"Another wave will fly by soon," Poe said, adjusting his lenses and turning the tubes of his telescope this way and that, trying to get the angle just right.

"Amazing!" Frank said, his jaw hanging open with delight.

"It's, like, the best fireworks display ever!" Len agreed.

Another bunch of meteors shot across the
sky, and the whole gang oohed and aahed.

"Except without all the blowing up," Misery
pointed out. "I feel much safer."

"I bet it would be totally cool to ride one of
those as it streaked through the sky! *Zoooooom!*
Pretty awesome!" Iris said, zipping her hand like
a comet before them.

"It does indeed fill one with awe," Poe said,
nodding.

"Oh, yes," Scaredy Bat said. "And now that I
know they're not alien ships coming to abduct
us, well . . ."

The others looked over at Scaredy Bat hopefully.

"Actually," Scaredy Bat went on, "they're still pretty scary."

Ruby smiled at him and put an arm around his shoulder. "You're safe with us, Scaredy Bat."

They all took turns looking through Poe's telescope at the amazing spectacle.

"There may not be another meteor shower like this in our lifetimes," Poe pointed out. "We're quite fortunate."

"I don't know," Iris said after her turn stargazing. "I almost wish it had really been an alien invasion. Now *that* would be an adventure."

Skull Boy nodded. "You must be *really* disappointed, Ruby," he said.

"Why, Skull Boy?" Ruby asked. She closed one eye tight to take her turn looking through the telescope. "This is incredible!"

"But all those doom cakes!" Skull Boy said. "All that decorating you did."

"Yeah," Iris added. "You spent all that time and worked so hard to make sure everything would be ready."

Misery nodded. "Right, Ruby," she said. "The aliens aren't coming, so there won't be a party."

Frank and Len, looking quite sad, nodded in agreement. "Just imagine," Len said. "All those desserts and decorations, gone to waste!"

"Such a tragedy!" Frank added, falling to his knees. "Oh, the humanity!"

Ruby laughed. "Oh, I don't know," she said. "I think a 'Meteor Shower of the Century' party sounds like a pretty good idea, too."

The gang all followed Ruby as she led them back into the Great Hall. And when they got there, they gasped with wonder. Orange and yellow streamers soared across the high ceilings. Hundreds of colorful doom cakes lined

the dining table at the far end of the room.
And dozens of tall pedestal candles, sparkling
brightly, filled the room with light.

"Wow, Ruby," Skull Boy said. "You sure did a
great job getting this party set up!"

"Yeah!" Frank said, rushing over to the
snacks table.

Doom Kitty, covered in paint and flour and
candle wax, harrumphed quietly and fell asleep
in the corner. "Well, I had some great help,"
Ruby admitted, smiling at her cat.

"Bang-up job, Ruby," Len agreed, shoving a doom cake into his mouth.

"It is a delightful party, Ruby," Poe agreed. "Surely the soiree of the season." He scratched his head and looked at the big banner hanging over the fireplace. It read, in big yellow, orange, and black letters:

WELCOME, OUT-OF-THIS-WORLD FRIENDS!

"But who will be your honored guests?" Poe asked, stroking his chin. "There are no aliens."

"The honored guests are already here!" Ruby pointed out with a giggle. "All of my greatest friends—they're all out of this world!"

And with that, the gang gathered around the huge window in the Great Hall, with punch and doom cakes and friends, to watch the greatest meteor shower of the century.

Dear Friend,

It was pretty funny that we all thought Poe
was an alien! It would have been amazing to meet
visitors from another planet, but I had just as much
fun watching the meteor shower with my friends.
Astronomy is a fun hobby to do with friends—you
should try it! Get a group together and search the
sky for stars, planets, and spaceships. But don't get
discouraged if you don't find an alien ship. It's like
I always say, there are big ships and there are small
ships, but the best ship is friendship.

Well, that's it for now. But my friends and I
have had many more adventures, and I can't wait to
share them all with you!

Your friend,

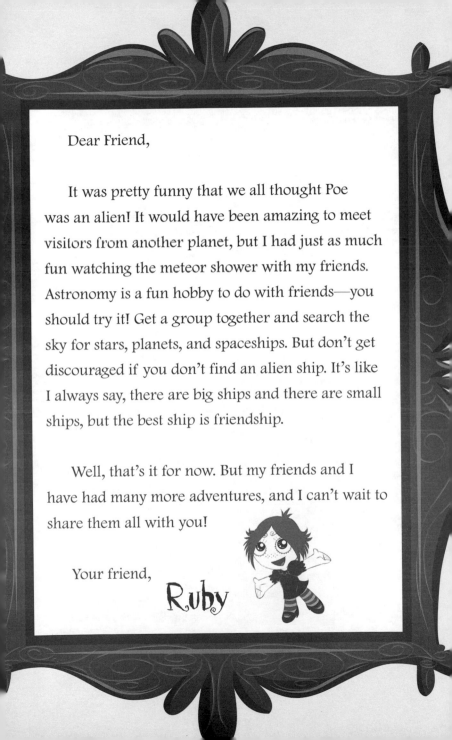

Ruby